Praises
Marvela and the ...

D0839170

Author Kathy Ellis reaches new heights in her very moving political poetic novella Marvela and the Broken Waters. Ms. Ellis, an Atlanta-based poet, educator, and language specialist, seeks to answer the question, "Why few influencers and armchair politicians are not talking about the destruction of Latin America in the the age of conquest." She writes: "Riches flow out of South America's many Caribbean outlets onto invading foreign vessels. European empires cross the Atlantic to carve the collateral like a Sunday feast." Ms. Ellis's novella, prose poem *Marvela and the Broken Waters* is about time shifts and the destruction of Latin America.

-Michaelangelo Rodriguez
Author "Return to Delaware Shore"
now streaming on Prime Time

Who better to investigate the literary underwater world of Mermaids than a griot herself, Kathy Ellis. We are channeled into a deep warm ocean of life; it is more than a visionary experience, the well-placed graphic descriptions allow us to taste, touch, and smell this water world...

What struck me were the well-defined settings. The story is a cross cultural undertaking in indigenous cultures in the New World and the African tribal nations. One cannot help but fall in love with the protagonist Marvela. Marvela has power, purpose, and prowess. What a gal! [*Marvela and the Broken Waters*] reminds me of Jamaican folklore.

-Carol Douglas-Welter, DPO
A two-time Kennedy Award nominee for Dramaturgy

Marvela and the Broken Waters is a book within a book, challenging and engaging readers of all ages. Challenging because Marvela reminds us of the savage historical tale of slave families torn asunder, of the loss of human dignity and freedom, and the plunder and cruelty of humankind. It would be enough to re-tell that tale. And yet (and yet!) the author ponders an important question: How is repair possible at this point? And the answer is well worth reading as Marvela and Miriwawu lead us across the broken waters to our true homes.

-Steven Owen Shields
author of *Creation Story and Daimonion Sonata*

Marvela
and the
Broken Waters

By Kathy Ellis

Acknowledgements

A steadfast partner and editor, David Hutto.

Helen Larson for sending a digital post card that ignited the imagination.

Johns Creek Poets for the ekphrastic writing prompt that inspired two mermaids.

BookLogix Publishers for saying *yes*.

Kristina Longacre for the book cover design and illustrations.

You, the reader.

In honor of the
International Mermaid Society

...Riches flow out of South America's many Caribbean outlets onto invading foreign vessels. European empires cross the Atlantic to carve the collateral like a Sunday feast while importing their diseases. Slave brokers and nationless pirates steal souls and gold. Conquistadores order the native archers to take aim at aggressors from other lands. For three centuries, over 12 million

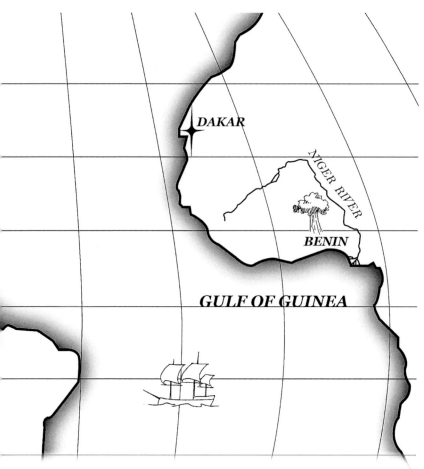

slaves from West Africa have been stacked like cargo for the grueling middle passage. Some must carry stones beyond their weight in the melting sun to build the Castillo San Felipe de Barajas, one of the finest forts in the Spanish empire. The mammoth fortress serves as one such bleeding artery, keen on the systemic culturicide of native civilizations that existed for thousands of years...

Wave 1

Marvela
of Aguamadria

In the midst of seahorses, oysters of black pearls,
sea plumes parading majestic swirls,
Marvela, mermaid of Aguamadria,
flashes her glittering fan in her empire's warm
currents.

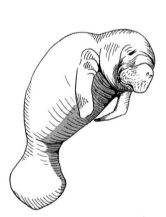

Sinuous dolphins and wise manatees
glide beside Marvela.

She possesses large, upturned eyes
     of dark jade,
bronze skin with intricate lace of henna shade,
and waves of mint-green tresses
that linger and flow.
Metallic bangles embrace her wrists.

Precious metals and other treasures
from sunken Spanish galleons,
nestle in the sandy floor of the vast Caribbean Sea.
    In the center of her secret water garden,
    a tall tree of barnacles and coral
    rises from the sea carpet toward the rays
        of the waking dawn.
Come the menagerie of colorful jewels:
angelfish, emerald urchins, damselfish,
and crimson sponges,
embraced by outstretched branches
softened by algae.
Translucent jellyfish surround the ocean tree
like bursts of violet fireworks.
    A large sea star drifts like a graceful dancer.
    The sea star's bold chakras of liquid light
    absorb the ripples and peril
    of the Outerworld's might.

The tropical creatures witness the mermaid
passing over the gallery of stolen heirlooms,
scattered under a veil of seaweed.
Marvela delights in the calm waters she leads.
May no evil enter Aquamadria lest it
feels her wrath like a typhoon of electric eels.

Wave II

Murmurs
from West Africa

Within Aguamadria,
lie cursed shipwrecks with endless streams
of pilfered Incan gold and silver,
emeralds from Boyacá,
lapis lazuli from the Andes.
Later came tobacco, cacao, indigo, sugar cane,
from sweltering fields,
on the backs of captured bones and moans
of West Africa.

Eclipses ago,
Marvela arose from the spirit of land priestesses,
who reigned along the spinal cord of the Andes Mountains.

Under the spell of a powerful Incan Shaman,
        Marvela comes to thwart the Spanish
        salvaging the new world riches-
        like an amphibian moving from land to water,
she swims from the Amazonian village of Iquitos,
into the spidery river network
toward the comfort of the wide-open sea.

Marvela takes to the water's consoling silence,
trusting the sonars of marine creatures
to reveal any evils entering Aguamadria.
The mermaid immerses
in the life-giving power of her domain
like a mother's womb.

Marvela understands her mission.
She spots the water graves where sunken galleons lie,
flicks her fishtail like an exotic eel
among the denigrated ships
and carries sacred artifacts
to the center of Aquamadria.

> Deft fingers hook
> pre-historic clay vases, ornaments, ancient quipus
> between barnacles and corals
> of the mauve-tinted tree.
> She hangs bright coins, copper,
> and exquisite body ornaments
> until the enchanting tree in the secret garden
> barely ebbs with the surge of tides.

Bars of melted gold-
that once beheld proud artisans' work-
lie tumbled around the tree.
Suddenly, the wind shifts.
Marvela emerges above the lapping waves
toward the stretch of another continent.
She lifts her magical conch to her ear

to savor the African whispers
of Yoruba, Ewe, and Igbo.
A chorus of beating drums murmurs.
It is time.

At long last, she hears from her African sister-siren.
Miriwawu is setting forth across the Atlantic guided
by unseen and visible powers.

> Marvela drapes her serene sapphire blanket,
> around the treasures of history, holding
> the plunder of souls in memory.

The mermaid waits.

Wave III

Miriwawu of the Niger River

The West African mermaid rests the large conch
on a nearby rock
along the calm shoreline
of the Bay of Guinea at Benin,
near what was once The Kingdom of Dahomey,
where the named became nameless
upon the forced walk around The Tree of Forgetfulness
and then chained and packed on suffocating vessels.

Her Incan sister-siren, Marvela,
received the final word through echoes of the shell.
Miriwawu strokes the small cloth bag around her neck of
       Orishas beads,
       traces of Islamic scriptures,
       colorful seashells.

Miriwawu's fishtail contains geometric shapes, colored
> burnt orange and muted red for the sun and sands
> of arid land,
> yellow for the cacti roses,
> green for the richness of the savannahs.
Beaded lace covers her face of ebony tones
with grave eyes.

The most powerful Nganga from a village
along the Niger River,
graces Miriwawu with a necklace of miniature bells
of spirits from both worlds.
To keep her direction across the vast ocean,
he places a glorious crown of gold and coral
topped by the North Star,
over her cascading raven locks.

Miriwawu is a lioness among gazelles
but takes to the salt of the sea like a chief's spear,
toward Dakar, Senegal, her port of departure.

The Nganga calls upon the depths of the ocean
for Yemanja, the powerful goddess of water,
to keep watch over Miriwawu.
He blesses the mermaid
with encounters of the divinity,
knowing that blessed spirits are infinite.

Indeed, Miriwawu will need much power.
The Griot, a regal woman, the storyteller and scribe
of the magnificent tribal histories in West Africa,
bestows the mermaid with extra strength
and deep wisdom.
But the Griot well knows the horrors.
Stories tell of the countless European and Arab invasions
of the African continent.
Shameful stories that tell of Africans selling Africans
to the highest bidders.

Hundreds of feet pound the dry African earth
to reclaim what was taken,
answered by the rhythmic drums and the masks
of ancestors from faraway villages,
all to wish Miriwawu well on her journey
and her safe return.
A serpent loosely wraps around her neck and chest
for protection from vicious humans and water animals.

Miriwawu's powers are to bring home
the one million Africans
who perished at sea over hundreds of years.
        Chattel bodies thrown off ships.
        Proud tribal leaders and their villagers who
        preferred suicide by water to bondage by land.
The dauntless mermaid and her spirit creatures-
        loggerhead turtles, a white crane, and a blue whale,
        the largest heart creature on Earth-
will gather the remains, spirits, and souls along
the cursed slave routes.

Wave IV

A Long
Time Coming

Marvela senses deep energy
from the air, sun, and ways of the water.
The large white wings of Miriwawu's spirit crane
appear on the wide horizon.
Marvela's dolphins are exuberant, splashing,
weaving in the waves,
and nudging her off the rock along the island shoreline.
Marvela sings of happiness in her native language
          of Quechua.
Nautical miles away, Miriwawu lifts her trusted conch.
After agonizing centuries,
she relishes Marvela's melodic songs of welcome.
Miriwawu returns the sentiment of songs in Igbo.
Her eyelids close as she swims toward
the velvety waters of the Caribbean.

As Miriwawu enters the sacred waters
          of Aguamadria,

she is embraced by a soothing light.
Marvela reaches for Miriwawu's warm hands
to guide her toward the center of the secret garden,
where Marvela and her guardians,
gathered the restless spirits and souls
tethered in the depths.

Miriwawu's ancient tortoises,
who witnessed the long-ago horror of slave ships
and the enslaved,
encircle the embracing sister-mermaids.

The wisdom of the tortoises
beholds such a glorious moment of the water world.
Thousands of liberated voices,
in a hundred mother tongues,
chant in unison their joy.

Miriwawu tenderly places a friendship necklace
of amber and quartz around Marvela's neck.

Marvela touches the crystals, knowing that one mission
      is near complete.
Marvela honors her African sister with Incan delights
of gold relics and emeralds
for her talisman on the perilous journey back
      across the Atlantic.
The salt of the water blends with the depth
      of Marvela's tears
as her tail splashes farewell,
plunging into the deep underworld
followed by her comforting animals.

Wave V

The Mecca of
All Lost Stories

The rays of the full moon
caress the African mermaid and her special convoy
as they maneuver the undercurrents, head winds,
and evil forces
along the nightmarish slave routes back
        across the Atlantic Ocean.
Miriwawu's miniature bells from the Nganga guide her
toward thousands more unfound souls,
drifting in the purgatories of the ocean
along the coasts of the Americas.
Yemanja, the water goddess, is keeping all
dangerous animals at bay
throughout the many valleys across the Atlantic.
The spirit animals possess innate abilities to uncover
more remains of the afterworld,
while Miriwawu unlocks their enslaved chains of pain.

So overwhelming is the painful energy
        of the dead's wailing,
that Miriwawu's extraordinary strength, indeed,
        begins to crumble.
The terrors of the enslaved engulf the dear mermaid,
crushing her own spirit.

Miriwawu loses breath that neither her serpent nor bells
are able to repel this invasion.

Saltwater overtakes her lungs.

Her eyes no longer blink.

She splashes her tail in frantic motion.

The blue whale's eyes respond in alarm.

Quickly, he attempts to balance Miriwawu on his dorsal fin.

From faraway, Nganga chants over the smoldering herbs...

"Miriwawu, the heavenly stars do not abandon you,
but to snap the iron bands of sorrow,
to survive like sculpted driftwood at sea.
The invisible threads of infinite power will
forever be by your side.
Do not give up, my special one."

The goddess mermaid and her noble blue whale
        feel a lightening jolt
of unexplainable reawakening from a greater pulse.
The tensions release, breathing returns.
Miriwawu slowly regains her strength
to guide the exhausted fleet
of returning spirits to safer waters.

They align with the magnetic draws of the Milky Way
as the wonderment flourishes brighter and grander,
while the ensemble heads east.
The night sky releases a million stars
to shower each returning soul with drops of silver.

From the view of distant darkness,
an immense swirl of stardust and diamonds
hovers over the shores and into the warm arms
of Mother Africa.

Sunrise replaces darkness,
an enormous stream of the returned
reaches the long shores with drums and jubilations.
The dancing masks call their ancestors while
thousands of feet dance the earth, dust rising into the sky.
The Nganga casts healing praises to the divinity, blessing
    Miriwawu,
    her valiant sea animals,
    Marvela,
    forgotten spirits of tribal kingdoms,
    Yemanja,
    joyful voices of the returned.

From the highest hilltop,
the Griot witnesses an incredible feat
of the entire West Africa.
The sheer blessings of life surround the grand Griot,
like a cloak of rare mystery.

Unfathomable grief,
as sharp as barb wires of a holocaust,
rejoicing spirits surpass the immoralities
of mankind.
The storyteller sheds her quiet tears
that behold the mecca of all-found stories.
To share with future generations,
the tales that future poets sing.

Wave VI

Marvela's Morning Song

The Milky Way streams over Marvela
like light and water through gills.
The mermaid basks in the blessings
of Miriwawu and the souls
safe in the maternal embrace of their homeland..

As the Milky Way disappears into the skies,
Marvela witnesses the ripples of a dusty sunrise.
She must return to the village of Iquitos on the Amazon,
to share the epic ventures with the village Shaman.
Underwater current maneuvers her toward
the shipwrecks' memories and treasures.
Shiny metals embody dark colonial secrets
and reflect the cruelty against native souls.

The mermaid's heart bids a most sad farewell
to her devoted dolphins and manatees.
She sings the soft lullabies that only sea guardians know,
Then, she is swallowed by the winding channels
of thick river grasses.

The Incan Shaman with all his mighty power
beckons three civilizations from the early breaths
of the Earth
for their best divers from the underworld.

      Aztecs of Tenochtitlan,

      Mayans of Tulum,

      Incas from Tacna,

warriors of worlds that ended.

The strong divers plunge in multitudes to return
      gold, silver, precious stones,
      symbols of stolen culture,
      to restore the roots of ancient civilizations.
Their magic transports copious loads of metals
and artifacts back to,
      Taxco and Guanajuato, Mexico,
      Castilla de San Felipe de Barajas in Colombia,
      and down the intricate river networks
      toward the Andes.

May the spirits slumber in peace
amongst the waves,
    and rest deeper than the roots
    of any islands.
It is true that many of the ghosts no longer
rise and wade in the oceans,
    but seawater remembers what it holds...

About the Author

Marvela and the Broken Waters is Kathy Ellis's third book of poetry. Kathy always had poetry dancing in her head and finally began putting pen to paper in 2014. Since then, Kathy has published in various online venues, journals, and magazines and has received numerous awards for her poetry. By profession, Kathy is a language coach for second language speakers and an intercultural communication trainer. Kathy resides in Atlanta, Georgia and hosts an international bed and breakfast with her two multilingual cats.

Keep Marvela swimming for humanity in the healing waters by liking and following her Facebook page, *Marvela and the Broken Waters*. Your reviews and comments are much appreciated. You will find questions for group discussions and the link to purchase *Marvela and the Broken Waters*.

Author's email
marvelabrokenwaters@gmail.com

About the Illustrator

Kristina Longacre is a multidisciplinary artist with a focus on painting and illustration. She graduated from the University of Cincinnati with a degree in Architecture and uses her design background in the work she creates. Much of her work explores themes of nature with bold colors. Kristina can be contacted at longacre.kristina@gmail.com.

Books may be purchased at BookLogix, Amazon, and Marvela's Facebook page. Contact your library and nearest bookstore to order a book.